"Hi-ya!"

Special thanks to Tiffany Stone—the nicest ninja I know

Text and illustrations © 2014 Chris Tougas

Owlkids Books acknowledges the financial support of the Canada Council for the Arts, the Ontario Arts Council, the Government of Canada through the Canada Book Fund (CBF) and the Government of Ontario through the Ontario Media Development Corporation's Book Initiative for our publishing activities.

Published in Canada by
Owlkids Books Inc.
10 Lower Spadina Avenue
Toronto, ON M5V 2Z2

Published in the United States by
Owlkids Books Inc.
1700 Fourth Street
Berkeley, CA 94710

Library and Archives Canada Cataloguing in Publication

Tougas, Chris, author, illustrator

    Dojo daycare / Chris Tougas.

ISBN 978-1-77147-057-5 (bound)

    I. Title.

PS8589.O6774D65 2014   jC813'.54   C2014-900337-4

Library of Congress Control Number: 2014932635

The text is set in Bang Whack Pow.
Edited by: John Crossingham and Karen Li
Designed by: Alisa Baldwin

Manufactured in Shenzhen, China, in April 2014, by C&C Joint Printing Co.
Job #HO0173

A   B   C   D   E   F

 Publisher of Chirp, chickaDEE and OWL
www.owlkidsbooks.com

DOJO
DAYCARE

Chris Tougas

Owl
kids

When ninja moms and ninja dads
Leave their hidden ninja pads,
They drop their children off to play
At Dojo Daycare for the day.

Shoes removed, the children bow
When **suddenly**—

Little ninja girls and boys
Fighting over ninja toys.
Pulling, pushing, tugging, taking,
Punching, kicking, busting, breaking.

It's a full-blown ninja riot.
Master claps and calls out,

"QUIET!"

"It's time for you to all reflect
On honor, kindness, and respect."

The Master sounds the gong. **Ka-BONGGG!**

Lunch is served, but things go wrong.
Before they gobble down their chow,
The dojo **shakes—**

Little ninjas all competing
Over plates and cups and seating,
Tipping chairs and acting rude,
Fighting over ninja food.

"It's time for you to all reflect
On honor, kindness, and respect."

"We're going to read a story now."
When **suddenly**—

No one listens to the Master.
Story time is a disaster.
Little ninjas throwing fits,
Wrecking books with ninja kicks.

Master can't control the riot.
Then...one little voice yells,

"QUIET!!!"

"It's time for us to all reflect
On honor, kindness, and respect."

Every ninja understands,
And fists turn into helping hands
As little ninjas work as one,
Undoing all that they have done.

Together ninja girls and boys
Stack the books and store the toys.
They clean the dojo through and through,
Until it looks as good as new.

The little ninjas give a bow.
Master bows and whispers...

When ninja kids and moms and dads
Go back home to ninja pads,

They share some laughs and have a bite
And wash and brush and hug goodnight,

Then backflip into comfy beds
And rest their sleepy ninja heads.

All is calm—at least for now.
Tomorrow? **Well...**

"Bye-ya!"

Wellfleet Public Library
55 West Main Street
Wellfleet, MA 02667
508-349-0310
www.wellfleetlibrary.org